Soulmates

A Thumb Adventure Novella

A THUMB ADVENTURE NOVELLA

ISBN: 9798664645576
Imprint: Independently published ©Copyright and all rights
reserved by: Greg Haughton. 2020

This book Soulmates of War is dedicated to Patricia de Leon de la Rosa, thank you for being extremely patient with me while I was writing this book. It is written with the idea of her being Maria, strong willed; full of energy and with a never-give-up attitude towards life.   I am so proud of her, she growing up so fast and strong the same as I also see Maria's strength developing.

To Jose Montelongo, who I imagined as General Klein, a very robust man, "Perro Sato". Thanks to him for the long chats on how both sides suffered so much during the war, and especially during the cold winter surrounding the Battle of the Bulge.

I cannot omit the wonderful people of Folkestone, Kent, in England, who put up with me while I investigated everything to do with WWII, the Grand Burstin Hotel, whose many guests were in fact WWII veterans and without their stories this book would not have its depth.

So, dedications done with, so start reading, hopefully you'll enjoy it, and remember your soul mate is out there somewhere.

PROLOGUE

During the Second World War there have been many stories told of happenings that have been strange, unbelievable and unexplainable. One of these stories has been fabled by many as the main reason why the Second World War came to an end when it did.

D-Day happened in the middle of June 1944 when, very quickly the Allied forces took back control of the French coastline. By the beginning of July, the Port of Cherbourg was almost back to normal business; shops were reopening and cafes and bars were being quickly filled with English soldiers, travelling through the French port on their way to the front line. Cherbourg had become a small, welcome stop that would take away, even just for a day, the stress of the war.

Little did anyone know that Germany was making plans to take back what was lost, to make an offensive push on French/Belgium coastline and the British Isles.

Even though it had only been two weeks after the invasion of Normandy, "D-Day", Germany lost a lot of ground and had had to retreat and regroup. They knew that they might even lose Paris, but believed it would only be a short while before they would take back everything. Therefore, strategically Germany was placing all their bets on this one final battle - "The Battle of the Bulge".

This all took place in the region around Ardennes on the French Belgian border

CHAPTER 1 THE MEETING

She felt his hand gentle on her cheek and as his lips touched hers, she had never felt so warm inside. His strong arms firmly enveloped her, wrapping around her waist. She was about to resist, but she knew that his strength would hold any struggle so; she gave in to him and bent her back slightly towards his lean body. By now his lips had dropped down towards her neck and electricity coursed through her entire body. Wrapping her arms around his neck, more for balance rather than wanting, she felt her own strength surge from within and wanted crush him into her bosom. Grabbing his face in her small hands she looked longingly into his intense eyes and violently kissed…

"Where were you?" asked her friend.

The rapturous feeling instantly dissolved as Maria's friend snapped her from her daydream.

"Nowhere special, I was just lost for a second" she replied, trying to sound nonchalant.

Wiping her hand down her slightly damp neck, Maria looked at her friend, frowned slightly, and then glanced over her friend's shoulder at the soldier sitting at a table in the café across the street. Maria had seen him several times over the last three days but had never been closer than they were right now. The first day she had been sitting quietly having lunch when she saw him leaving the mess hall. He had been having lunch with other soldiers and his smile had been captivating.

The following day she had seen him again, he had come into the infirmary and without waiting he had been ushered into an office with a doctor. His rank had given him a little push in the right direction; the doctor had asked for a nurse to help out, however, she had been busy with another soldier. She found out later that he had come in to have stitches removed from a training injury he had received in England. The nurse who had to help out made a big issue of how handsome he was and the word "captivating" was used again for his smile.

Maria was quite sad to find out that she would be going back to England shortly and unfortunately, the soldier was going to the front line the following day.

Luck had played into her hands though; it was now that she was standing just across the street from him. He sat calmly talking with two other soldiers in his crisp, clean uniform of a ranking officer. Maria wasn't sure what rank he was, but she could see from where she was standing, the medal strip on his jacket. He looked comfortable, relaxed and carefree; sipping occasionally from a cup which she assumed was coffee.

Maria hadn't realised she was staring at him; but one of his companions had and leaned discreetly towards him whispering. He looked over in Maria's direction. When their eyes met there was an explosion in Maria's stomach, something she had only felt in her daydreams. His eyes were alive and his dark hair matched their colour. She looked harder and saw everything within their toasted brown colour. He smiled at her and for a fleeting moment, the world stood still.

People have witnessed that time slows down when love at first sight flashes between two people. Time for Maria and the soldier almost stopped. The car about to pass by totally paused on its way down the street, the man flicking a cigarette butt out of the car window, the girl selling flowers on the corner had a pleading look on her face, trying to sell a bunch of daisies to a passing couple, a dog barking at a cat climbing a drainpipe. Nothing moved but their beating hearts.

The soldier moved, Maria moved past her friend, whose smile was frozen, and moved across the pavement towards him. The soldier stood up, and moved towards her and then crossed the street, Maria waited for him to cross and never for an instant broke eye contact. She felt lighter and the slight smile on his face made the hairs on her arms stand as if the atmosphere was charged with electricity. Then, there he was, directly in front of her; she looked up into his laughing eyes and timidly smiled, then he said, "Hello."

Everything started up again, the people started walking down the street and some others continued their conversations in the cafés along the street. Maria didn't notice any of these things as she was lost in his world. What Maria didn't know was that the soldier was also lost in her world.

Without Maria knowing he had actually seen her several days earlier, she hadn't seen him, he had been with two soldiers when they were getting their initial medical check-up on arrival in Cherbourg. It was standard procedure for every officer before they left for the front line. When he had seen Maria he wanted to meet her and but just as he was about to be called by her another nurse entered and told her that her help was needed at an emergency. She left immediately, leaving him feeling hollow and looking into the eyes of a new nurse smiling at him. Later on he had tried to find her again, but he did not even know her name which made things even more difficult. He had seen her briefly again the following day in the mess hall, she had sat down with her lunch at the other end of the hall large room and he was about to stand and take the opportunity to introduce himself when his friends had risen at the same time and jokingly moved him towards the door. He thought that she had briefly looked in his direction and just when he was about to wave, she had lowered her gaze to her meal. Now, he hadn't noticed at all until his friend called his attention to a nurse staring at him from across the street, he looked up to find himself absorbed in her gaze.

The afternoon in Cherbourg was the beginning of a new day, when Maria met her soldier.

He spoke softly, "I would like to say just one thing to you: If the war could be won with beauty, you would have won it the it began.

Maria listened to his words, the tilt and accent of each syllable mesmerised her. Maria smiled.

"Thank you sir, that's very kind of you to say that, but if it weren't for the war we wouldn't be having this conversation would we?"

His smile broadened even more and introduced himself. "My name's Anthony, it's a pleasure to meet you Maria."

Surprise lit up Maria's face. "You know my name, sir?" Searching his face for some clue as to where he could have found out her name.

His smile showed smooth white teeth. "It was quite easy really, it is written on the folder you are carrying in your arms."

Maria quickly glanced at the folder she had been using as a shield to hide her embarrassment and when she realised that her name, which was blazoned in bold black letters on the folder, she hid it carefully behind her and smiled back at Anthony.

"I have seen you a few times at the hospital with your friends and to be quite honest, I have been entranced by your beauty." He quickly mentioned to break the awkward silence. "I haven't been able to keep my eyes off you. What is it that makes you so magical?" he continued.

"Sir, you are making me blush with your kind words." Maria replied coyly, a crimson smudge appearing on her cheeks.

"Will you be going to the front line, Anthony?" she asked him, slightly changing the topic.

It was the first time Maria had spoken his name and to be quite honest, it sounded subtly sweet on her lips. When

Anthony registered the use of his name it gave him goose bumps, the hairs on his arms briefly stood on end. They continued talking for a short while longer, small amounts of valuable information that sparked much more than a fire within them.

"I don't quite recognise your accent sir?" Maria asked Anthony trying in vain to guess his place of birth.

"I wasn't born in England but in Australia. I came to England very young to get an education. My parents sent me to school and University and I must admit that I have stayed with my family all over England. Therefore, my accent isn't defined."

Anthony was looking at Maria's face while he was talking and smiled even more at her beauty. He continued with a question for her.

"And you Maria are you French or English? Your accent has a definite 'je ne sais quoi.'

"Yes, my mother is French, from Paris, and a nurse like myself, she is back in London with my father, he's English, and they met during the First World War He owns a metal factory and obviously runs it now for the war effort making spare parts for the British and American military vehicles."

The conversation continued still standing on the corner on the street in Cherbourg.

Life continued around them, but neither of them noticed as they were both lost in

their own new world.

Suddenly, they were stolen from each other. Anthony's friends had come over and told him that they had to return to the barracks, as did Maria's friends, saying that they had to leave and pack the suitcases before returning to London. Both Maria and Anthony were startled by the unwelcome intrusion and were instantly sad as the realisation of parting, perhaps forever, overcame them.

"I would like to correspond with you while I am on the front line, my family writes to me, but it would be nice to hear stories from someone I like very much" Anthony said, quite sure of the fact that she would say yes. Their conversation had been intense and there was an urgent mental and physical desire to continue.

As his friends had reached the end of the street and completely disappeared around the corner, Anthony finally broke off the conversation, "I have to go, please could I write to you then?" he pleaded with her, scribbling something in pencil and handing it to her.

"Yes, of course, I would love to hear from you." She replied, "I can't wait to hear from you, I'll write to you as well." Maria wrote her details on a small piece of paper she had in her folder.

Throughout the fifteen minute conversation they had never touched, they had respectfully maintained the correct distance society required of people getting to know each other for the first time. Yet, Anthony leaned over and lightly kissed Maria on her cheek. It was as if lightening had struck, a huge invisible spark jumped between them, cheek to cheek, it made them jump. Both rubbed their cheeks, and they smiled and laughed a little at the strange phenomena. Anthony slid his hands down Maria's sleeved arms, sliding past the starch white cuffs. He grabbed her hands in his own, Maria had dropped her folder on the floor and took a strong hold of his hands too. She realised that her heart was beating so fast that she could hear it pounding in her ears. The intensity between them grew to such strength that both their breaths were caught within an almost childlike laughter. Cautiously they leaned in towards each other again and, quite carefully this time, made contact. Maria felt his cleanly shaved skin and noticed a light smell of aftershave. Anthony felt her soft skin and inhaled her perfume, a perfume scent that he would never forget.

Anthony forced himself to let go of Maria's hand and ran down the street, occasionally turning to wave goodbye.

He had written down on an old ration ticket his full name, rank and company. With this information any letter would arrive.   Maria folded it carefully and placed it in her purse. She lightly touched her cheek where the spark had hit and noticed that it was still tender to her touch.

CHAPTER 2   FIRST CONTACT

Only a few hours had passed when Maria decided to send Anthony a letter. She sat at the desk in her room at the hospital, imagining Anthony doing the same. She closed her eyes and creatively imagined him also sat at a desk; he stood up and moved around the room looking at a piece of paper in his hand, chewing on the back of a pencil. He had removed his jacket and Maria could see that his uniform was ruffled from the day's journey. She was really surprised at how vivid her imagination was. She saw every single detail as if it were real. She followed his steps around the room and saw that he was about to walk into the chair. Maria waited silently for her mind's eye to fill in the image and when he finally tripped over the chair she chuckled. Anthony silently cursed at his stupidity and Maria laughed out load. At that moment Anthony stopped what he was doing and looked around the room. Maria watched amusingly as Anthony walked around the room looking for something else, she saw him mouth out her name. Maria, shocked, opened her eyes and instantly felt tired, as if her thoughts had exhausted her. It was still only eleven o'clock in the morning, but it felt as if she had been awake for twenty four hours working a full day. She climbed back into bed and left the letter until later in the afternoon when she had rested.

Anthony was perplexed. His mind was filled with Maria and he wanted to write to her, now, laying his thoughts and feelings on paper. After all it would be difficult if not impossible when he reached the front line and he needed her to know how she made him feel, in case he never got the chance to tell her again. He removed his jacket, sat, picked up his pen, and stared at the blank sheet of paper and realised he did not know how to start. He began to pace the room, expressing ideas out loudly, chewing his pen, looking at the ceiling for inspiration and carelessly walked into a chair. He thought he heard a chuckle but when he cursed out loudly at the stabbing pain in his toe, he was certain he heard someone laugh. It was Maria laughing; it was her, he was sure of it.

"Maria?" he called out several times, he looked around the room and he had an eerie but distinct feeling of being spied on. "Maria, where are you?" and then without any warning the feeling was gone.

Anthony sat in his room wondering what had happened. After a short while he gave up his train of thought and returned his attention to the letter he was writing. It was a letter of joy at their meeting and a mixture of happy thoughts and wishing it had lasted longer. He told her that she had smelt of spring flowers and that her eyes had glowed honey coloured in the morning sun. His first impressions were all he had to write about and then he started telling Maria in his letter all the things he wanted in life. He sat daydreaming looking out of the window. He heard a rustling behind him and he turned to find himself looking at Maria lying in a bedroom that wasn't his own. He immediately recognised Maria fast asleep on the bed and jumped from his chair, which fell noisily to the floor. Anthony looked momentarily at the fallen chair and returned his gaze to the bedroom and Maria, but the image had gone and he found himself in his lonely bedroom. He slumped down on the chair and felt a sudden wave of fatigue. He felt as if he had run a marathon, he moved to lie on his bed and promptly fell into a deep sleep

CHAPTER 3   THE REASONING

Several hours later they both woke up. It had been one of the deepest sleeps either had ever had. Nothing had disturbed them; fortunately no one had knocked on their door and awakened them from their slumber. Fully refreshed and aware that the day had turned into late afternoon, both Maria and Anthony wondered about what had happened that morning. Maria sat quietly on the edge of the bed and relived what she had seen so clearly in her head. Anthony was also thinking about his vision, standing at the window, looking out over a small wood somewhere in the middle of France; he contemplated on how clearly he had seen Maria lying in her bed. It had been so real.

They both decided that they would try and get something to eat and simultaneously walked down the stairs grasping the banister at the same moment so as not to fall. Equally they entered their individual mess halls, picked up a tray and walked down the line. At the same time they arranged their cutlery in the same manner and after receiving their food sat at a table, same side and same place. The morsels on their plates disappeared into their mouths and were chewed at each other's rhythm. There were no napkins on the table and both of them retrieved a handkerchief from their pockets and purse to clean their mouths. Sips of coffee were taken from stained cups, two sugars, no milk. They stood and left their individual mess halls and walked out into a darkening sky.

Anthony was leaving the following morning for the front line barely twenty miles from where they were. He supposed that he wouldn't get much sleep after that so he returned to his room with the intention of continuing his letter to Maria. She had not left his thoughts in any way during his meal and he was looking forward to finishing it. He climbed the stairs wishing he would see Maria lying in his bedroom as he had seen her before.

Maria was also thinking of Anthony and like him, she had not thought of anything else during the meal. She had also returned to her room and was readying her bags for her return to England the following morning. She looked at the paper she was going to write on, the letter to Anthony, she moved towards it again with the intention of finishing it. She was looking forward to putting her thoughts and feelings on paper so that he would smile at her words.

Both walked to the papers on their desks and wrote their words and finishing their letters, placed them in their envelopes. It was getting late and, as if synchronised, decided to get some sleep. Maria thought of Anthony and Anthony thought of Maria just as they walked past the standing mirror in their bedrooms. Something caught their peripheral vision, Maria saw something dark brown instead of the blue and white she was wearing. They both caught these brief changes in colour and realised something was amiss. Their reflection was not their own. They had both walked past the mirror but they stopped at the same moment and returned. Incredulously they stared at each other, the silent image was as clear as if they were looking in the mirror. Maria lifted her hand and called his name. Anthony saw her mouth his name but could not hear what she was saying. They both realised that what they were seeing was in fact real. They moved closer to the mirror and rushed words and looked at each other up and down. Anthony showed Maria his letter without an address, she quickly showed him her letter which had her address on the reverse and he jotted it down.

Both stood there trying to comprehend what was happening to them when fatigue again started to creep in, they tried to concentrate on the mirror, the image was starting to fade and they were beginning to see themselves faintly in the mirror. Quickly Anthony motioned to Maria to write to him and she understood somehow that he wanted her opinion of this phenomenon they were living. She nodded her understanding and the image of Anthony disappeared. Both Maria and Anthony fell onto their beds and passed out from the effort. Just before they entered into their dream state, they both smiled at the miracle they were in. Anthony's sleep was filled with distant memories, 'transmission of information', 'communication between minds', 'feeling from a distance' and before he woke he had the answer – telepathy, and even the name of the man who had originally coined the word, Frederic Myers.

CHAPTER 4

THE CONNECTION GETS STRONGER

A couple of weeks passed during which Maria and Anthony had been continuously testing their new gift. It was very strange at first and also very tiring. They found it was easier to send thoughts, images and quick views of themselves in a mirror. Initially they used an old chalk boards to write messages and this way they learnt a lot about each other. Anthony's rank gave him many opportunities to be available. Connecting with Maria generally happened in the evenings as both of them ended up feeling exhausted. Anthony decided to record the duration of their connections and gradually he noticed their time together was lengthening. One day Maria reached out for Anthony and closing her eyes she imagined his shaven face and it filled out in her mind. She saw him without a mirror.

Their thought images, photographs so to speak, of their everyday lives. Good times and bad, Maria, shocked one day back in London, sent Anthony an image of the buildings destroyed by German "buzz bombs". He sent an image of injured soldiers coming back from the front line. Both of them after that seemed to notice each other's feelings of the war and stopped sending those types of images.

For some unknown reason to the British troops there was a brief respite in the fighting and whilst waiting for orders of further action Anthony took the opportunity to return for a few days leave to a small hamlet just a few hours away from the front line. He was given a room in a small auberge and frequently wandered the quaint village and to develop his connection with Maria. At the same time, feigning an illness, she Maria took leave and went to stay with family in Cambridge. She sat on the bank of the river Cam talking with Anthony. They had discovered that they could have short conversations, at first, mouthing out the words, and then they progressed to faintly hearing some words. Not long after this the sentences became longer and even though they were tired afterwards, they were able regain their energy without having to sleep for several hours. Anthony's leave would soon finish and although they were separate from each other they had in the short time concentrating on their gift become much closer. They both knew they were beginning to fall in love and were anxious for the next encounter. They were hungry to learn more about each other and they greedily consumed each other's words.

The few days they had together were amazing. Not only were they communicating with soft whispering voices but had discovered something new. It had been Anthony this time, Maria was asleep early one morning and Anthony had tried to connect with her, but as he reached out she became more solid, in fact he looked around and realised that he was standing in her bedroom, he looked at her as she slept. He noticed that he could do this without using too much energy, he felt that just being with her, but not connected with her, he could stay much longer. He walked around the sparsely furnished room, glancing every now and then at Maria on the bed. He accidently brushed the door and his arm passed through it. Snatching it back, firstly with shock, he tried again. Cleanly passing through the door he stood on the other side and stood looking amazedly at the dorm. There were few people around and those he did see obviously didn't see him. He wandered through to almost the other side of the dorms when he felt Maria waking. Then the strange thing happened, in the blink of an eye he was by her side again. He smiled at her waking up and stretching. He decided to leave before she showered and dressed, his gentleman rules were a lot stronger than his curiosity and he hoped his departure was before her awareness of him. As he broke contact he definitely noticed that he was not as tired as he normally would have been; interesting.

Maria returned to London that afternoon and although Anthony had to wait two days more to return to the front line, he kept an eye on Maria. He occasionally appeared nearby on the train down from Cambridge. She hadn't seen him, but he was sure she felt his presence. Once back in London Maria made her way to the hospital.

The Hospital of St John and St Elizabeth founded in 1886, a beautiful Victorian style building not directly in the centre of the city but close enough to major railway stations to be of a great benefit during air raids or badly injured soldiers coming back from the coast of England or even the front line. It had enormous underground operating theatres which made it even more important as the war persisted.

She walked into the offices at to see the director of the hospital slamming the telephone down and screaming as if that Hitler was to blame for everything, which in fact was true.

"What is the problem?" asked Maria trying to look helpful in some way. Mr. James looked up from the bunch of

26

papers stuck in his hand at Maria and asked her without expecting an answer.

"I suppose you couldn't drive an ambulance down to Trafalgar Square could you?" He returned his attention to the papers and continued without waiting for her to respond.

"I have no drivers, I have no surgeons and the war department is always asking for doctors here and there. What am I supposed to do, pull a driver out of thin air, knit one, produce one out of smoke?"

Maria looked at him with empathy, he looked as if he hadn't slept for three days and was about to have a nervous breakdown.

"I can drive the ambulance down for you; I am only a nurse though not a surgeon, if it's of any help?" she said quietly.

Mr. James stopped and looked at her incredulously, he couldn't believe his ears, yet, here stood a nurse in his doorway offering to help. He supposed that it wouldn't be that difficult, it was only fifteen minutes away from the hospital. Pick up the patients coming in on the train from the south coast and return.

"Alright, if you think you can do it, then here are the keys to the ambulance outside. Get some help loading the stretchers

27

and bring them back here safe and sound." Mr. James said in one breath, as he handed Maria the keys.

Hesitantly Maria smiled and made her way through the hospital and onto the forecourt where the ambulance was parked. Whilst the rolled up stretchers were being loaded she climbed behind the huge steering wheel, placed the key in the ignition, turned it and heard the huge diesel engine growl into life. Crunching the gear lever into reverse she realised that the ambulance was much heavier than the town car she had driven before the war. She had only been fourteen years old but her grandfather had taught her quite well and those skills were now coming in useful.

Handling the steering wheel with all her strength she pulled out of the hospital grounds and moved along the main street towards Trafalgar Square. There were very few cars now and the last blitz had left some streets unable to navigate, fallen buildings had totally blocked them and Maria had to follow detour signs for most of her journey. The diversions and alternative routes added an unwelcome forty five minutes to her journey.

Maria fairly quickly located the train carriage carrying the wounded and able-bodied soldiers helped load the ambulance with nine stretchers, four on each side and one on the floor. A nurse, who had accompanied the soldiers from the coast jumped in the passenger seat next to Maria.

"I want to go to the hospital with you to make sure they get there alright. I've been with them since we left Folkestone. Once they are at the hospital safe and sound then I'll go and spend a few days with my family in Oxford." The nurse seemed quite adamant about coming along and Maria didn't complain, in fact she was relieved to have company.

The ambulance eased out of Charing Cross Station and made its way passed past Trafalgar Square up towards Piccadilly Circus. Just then, sirens blared out all over London.

"Not now!" Maria screamed over the noise. "I can't believe my luck!"

The streets emptied rapidly as the entire population of London had done so many times before. The bleak looks on their faces showed fear, the tension in the air made things worse. It was unusual that a bombing raid would happen during the day and even stranger that the enemy planes had reached London. People were being hurried by frantic wardens pushing them into the shelter of the underground. The sirens kept wailing out over the city and above their noise she couldn't hear anything else. Fear gripped Maria and there was nothing she could do about it.

The few cars that were actually travelling the streets stopped in their tracks and the drivers either ran to a shelter or went down into the underground system. Maria couldn't stop. There was no way she could unload the stretchers, so she was left

with no other choice but to drive the rest of the way to the hospital.

By the time she got to Piccadilly Circus the streets were entirely empty. The driving did actually become easier but they were still twenty minutes away from the hospital. If her luck held she would make it there before anything serious happened. She was wrong though.

Flak cannons were the first thing she heard, then the bigger blasts of falling bombs. They weren't going to make it to the hospital in time. Maria's only thoughts were of Anthony.

Anthony had been given respite from the front line battles. The German soldiers had retreated back to the town and were licking their wounds and resting themselves. It would just be a few hours before the battles flared up again. He had refreshed himself in an officer's mess hall and had found a deserted farmhouse to get some well-earned rest. The farmhouse had been empty for a long while and obvious occupancy had happened from both sides. Slogans in both German and English had been written on the walls. The swastika had been painted over by both the allied forces, the combination of union jack and stars and stripes were brighter and good but couldn't quite cover the Nazi scrolling on the wall.

Anthony walked over to a rocking chair that seemed to be at least in some sort of reasonable condition, sat down and breathed deeply.

His thoughts of Maria had never left his mind and again he found himself wanting to feel her in his mind. However, he refrained from doing it because they had both discovered that it tired them considerably. Since the last time they had made a strong connection they had dabbled a little and their connection had become stronger, clearer and lasted longer. They knew, however, that afterwards they had to be totally free to rest and at this moment he felt that Maria needed to be alert.

His mind relaxed and was about to fall asleep when Maria's voice burst into his mind with such force it almost shook him out of the rocking chair. Anthony had never heard

Maria's voice so strong, they had barely heard each other and their voices had always been soft with very short conversations.

This was totally different. Anthony climbed back on the chair and concentrated.

"What is it Maria?" he quickly replied instantly in touch with her.

There was silence. Anthony asked again and was shown a scene in his mind's eye as they connected.

He found himself looking through Maria's eyes and she was struggling with a steering wheel. Swerving this way and that, an enormous explosion blew apart the street in front of them tearing to pieces the foundations of the building right next to the vehicle she was driving. In slow motion it started to tumble and fall into the street. Anthony saw through her eyes and felt that she was going to brake and knowing that it would be a fatal mistake, Anthony took control of Maria's mind and body, he made her stamp on the accelerator instead of braking, swerved the ambulance to one side avoiding the falling rubble. Anthony had no idea what he was driving but knew instantly that she was in real danger. He asked himself why she was out driving during a bombing raid in the middle of London.

All around them bombs were falling and Anthony steered Maria through all the dangerous parts, not a moment too soon, they were both getting tired. The hospital was still quite a distance away but it seemed like the immediate danger was over, Anthony pushed what little energy he had left into Maria and she felt him leave her.

She eventually arrived at the hospital with all nine passengers safe and sound. The other nurse asked some awkward questions regarding things she had said and the way she had driven. Maria shrugged off the questions as 'luck' and left it at that.

She walked over to her ward in the station and handed the keys with Mr James, he who looked at her incredulously,

"How did you drive through the attack?" he asked thinking that he was seeing a ghost instead of a nurse.

"I was lucky! Do mind if I go home as I feel quite tired?"

Mr. James just nodded his answer and watched Maria as she walked out of his office. He was still looking at the empty door when another nurse entered asking for supplies.

Early next morning Maria woke up feeling Anthony's presence. She opened her mind and let him in.

"Are you alright?" was his question.

"Yes, thank you for helping me yesterday; I wouldn't have been able to have done it without you."

"Yes you could have, you seemed to have been doing just fine until I took over." Anthony tried to keep his voice calm as he spoke to Maria. He didn't want her to get upset because of yesterday.

Throughout the rest of the day they would connect briefly and check on each other. Then later on that evening Maria spoke to Anthony.

"I have been thinking how to make our conversations better."

"How?"

"Do you remember the mirror the first day?"

"Yes. That was a surprise I can tell you." Maria continued. "Let's try to make a place here in our minds where we can see each other. But we have to imagine a place together." She closed her eyes.

"Do you remember the street we first met?"

"Yes I do." he replied.

In Anthony's mind he built the street and the café he was sitting at having a coffee. Maria built in her mind the corner she was standing on with her friend.

"Do you see it??" Anthony asked Maria.

"Yes, I have it. But I can't see you. Where are you?"

"I'm right here." his voice directly in her left ear. She turned to see his smiling face. It was sublime looking into his eyes, feeling the growing love they had for each other. Their voices seemed to have a slight echo and their images were ghostlike, semi- translucent but alive and in full colour.

Anthony reached out his hand and pressed against Maria's cheek but it passed straight through it. There was a surprised look on both their faces, they touched each other's hands and watched in amazement as they blended, one inside the other.

For ten minutes they talked animatedly about their adventures so far and unbelievingly about what was happening to them. They could feel that it took less energy this way; nevertheless it was Maria who first started to feel tired.

"Don't worry I'll be staying at home for the rest of the day. Will you be ok?"

"I'm away from the front line at the moment and won't have to go back until tomorrow. So there's no need for you to worry about me either."

"I can't hold the connection anymore Anthony, I'm sorry. I have to go. I love you!" she said making as to kiss him, even though she knew that she wouldn't be able to touch him.

The moment the words left Maria's mouth energy burst forth between them, they kissed and for a brief second, their lips connected with a burst of light, Maria felt Anthony's soul and warmth. Then just as fast as they felt this amazing energy it was gone. Both of them found themselves standing alone yet feeling very happy.

They struggled to stay awake but, overcome by fatigue, they slept, the last night before returning to the fight.

CHAPTER 5   THE TRIALS OF WAR!

A few weeks had passed and as the strength between them grew, other dangers were also avoided. Anthony asked for Maria's help one day. Intelligence was needed about a German Camp on the front line. Anthony needed to know how many soldiers there were in the camp and possible weak spots. Maria was perplexed as how she was able to do this but with his help she was able to go forth into their camp and look around. Anthony projected his energy into the camp, as she walked through it, saw their layout, weapon points and most importantly a latrine exit that was neither protected nor defended. With this knowledge they took 400 German soldiers prisoner and made a strong foothold on the frontline. Anthony was called back to headquarters to receive a promotion for this act. Maria saw the presentation through Anthony eyes and was so proud of him.

Of course, this time away from the frontline was also time they spent together. They became stronger and stronger, what was once minutes of connection were now as long as an hour and without becoming tired. Even with their increased power they were never able to touch each other again, no matter how hard they concentrated or willed it, and no contact was ever made. Time was flying by for both of them and rumours were rife that the end of the war was coming. There were also other rumours. Soldiers in Anthony's command started talking about strange happenings, how their newly appointed Major was always informed of things before they happened, of how he was seen talking to himself even though there was no one around. Maria was also looked upon as eccentric, originating from the nurse that had been in the ambulance with Maria, seeing how she had driven it with such force and conviction that it was almost supernatural. Other nurses had spoken of the times Maria had also been seen talking to herself.

Although only rumours, information of any type eventually reached German officials. Walter V. Reichenau, one of Hitler's generals received reports about Anthony's eccentricities and because he was interested in supernatural occurrences, Reichenau turned his attention towards the Major.

"What is it they say about this Major, Kurt?" Reichenau asked one of his many aides.

"It is said, mein General, that the Major speaks with a woman, he has been heard talking to a someone named Maria."

"Is it possible that he speaks with a Christian belief and is having conversations with the mother of Christ?"

"Nein, mein Herr, he is not a religious person as far as our source of information is aware. Apparently the major often isolates himself but returns with intelligence relating to our locations, arsenal, troops, our strengths and weaknesses and his company have taken control, knowing exactly when, where and how to strike. We no longer have an agent amongst them or we could eliminate him."

"I don't understand how this major can get this vital information, it seems like as if by magic. I have my most trusted aides in this front and though we are making good ground on the other fronts, here we are losing ground. We have almost been pushed back by the allied force and this unruly band of mercenaries is in the way of Hitler's final push on Ardennes. If we can break through here, take the port of Antwerp, then there will be a possibility of regaining France and winning this war."

"Yes, mein General. What is it you want me to do?" the aide stammered.

"I want you to find out more about this Major and this Maria. There is something we are missing."

The General was left pondering over maps and papers. Normally he would have had solved this puzzle by now as he had so many spies infiltrating the allied forces and even the upcoming military push by the Germans on Ardennes was not going to be stopped by the Allied forces from England. They may even force the Americans back across the English Channel, who knows, given time they would recover what they had lost and conquer the world. All for the Führer.

CHAPTER 6   BACK INTO THE ACTION

When Anthony arrived back at the front line nothing was happening, well, nothing had happened. However, all of a sudden all hell broke loose. It was if the Germans had been waiting for Anthony to come back, they attacked with such strength that it caught the British soldiers unexpectedly.

They rallied quickly enough, fighting off the first and second wave of Germans. Yet the third and final wave much stronger than the earlier strikes. Anthony was struggling to stop what few soldiers he had left from doing something rash like charging or even worse running away. Anthony screamed at them to hold their ground and face the enemy. They did so and they seemed to be holding back the tide of attacking Germans. It was just then, in the midst of the foray, that Anthony felt Maria's presence; he knew that his thoughts were betraying him and that was why she was here.

She stood behind him watching him fight, experiencing his intense thoughts of worry and fear, but it was not for himself it was for those in his command. He was defending them like a madman. German soldiers were falling over each other to attack them; screams in German echoed out over the field, they weren't screams of pain but of anger. What little German Maria understood seemed directed towards Anthony. She couldn't understand why. She looked at her beloved and saw him beginning to weaken, the fight was going out of him and each wave of Germans that came for them drained him a little more. In desperation she channelled her energy into him and he brightened, his strength revived and he fought harder. She heard him thank her quietly as he continued defending his post.

As the foray slackened Anthony was able to get his bearings, he sat on a box and was cleaning the dirt from his face when out of the corner of Maria's eye she saw a German soldier take aim from a corner of the trench where Anthony was sitting. Anthony hadn't seen him. The German was about to shoot. Maria screamed.

"Noooooooooooo!"

She pushed Anthony with all her energy. She placed her hands in front of her, palms facing away and fingers spread wide, she felt a force pulsing through her entire body, so she pushed it hard through her hands and aimed it at Anthony. It shot out of her hands and hit him full in the chest just as the

German soldier fired his weapon. Anthony was thrown backwards off the box with such force that his breath was knocked out of him, the bullet grazed the left shoulder of his jacket, ripping through the material and smacking into the post just behind him. After the blow Maria had given him he landed on the ground, rolling over onto one knee he pulled his revolver and shot the German soldier, knocking him off his feet.

At that moment he realised that it was Maria who had saved him, he connected with her and she smiled. He noticed that the effort of saving his life had taken every bit of energy she had had. Anthony told her to rest and he'd be in touch later.

The moment he felt that she had left his side he reached down and pulled a handkerchief from his pocket and pushed it inside his jacket. He cringed at the pain he felt where the bullet wound was. The whole thing had been very close; if it hadn't been for Maria he would probably have died.

He walked over towards the body of the German soldier he had shot, he had fallen behind a mound of earth but when Anthony got there, there was nothing but the rifle the soldier had been carrying.

CHAPTER 7   A SECRET UNCOVERED

His name was Peter Bauer, a German soldier who had been ordered to attack the British. He had also been told to look out for a British Major who was extremely lucky and often spoke to himself. Bauer had thought it very strange but followed orders. He had attacked and had made his way flanking the British soldiers, he had brought his rifle to bear and had aimed at the major but just as he was about to shoot he saw the major talking to himself and then amazingly, it appeared that an invisible force pushed him out of the way of his shot. Then the major had turned and shot him, he hadn't moved fast enough; the bullet hit him hard knocking him off his feet. His shoulder was now hurting more than ever more. The bullet had passed straight through and it felt like it was fire. He had made it back to the German trenches and was taken to see one of the officers.

Bauer started to tell his story to the ranking officer, but he was silenced until other officers arrived. Bauer had no idea why the other officers were there but he told his story nonetheless.

"He was pushed away from the shot, there was no one around to do any pushing but he was definitely pushed out of the way!" Bauer reported, finishing his story.

"Thank you soldier, go and get patched up and keep up the good work."

As Bauer left the room and made his way to the infirmary; he was wondering why this British officer was getting so much attention. He had the wound dressed and fell asleep, the next morning he had forgotten everything about it because the nurse found him dead lying face down in his bed. Bauer's body was ceremoniously dumped into a common grave behind the hospital tent.

The German officers, that same morning, were planning something different and it had nothing to do with the British Major. One of them placed an envelope on the desk. One of the officers opened it and read the contents. It seemed that there were several candidates. There were a few addresses in London, blazoned on the front, circled in red and marked to one side of them was just one word: "Kidnap".

CHAPTER 8   SOMETHING'S HAPPENING

It was the following day that Maria contacted Anthony again. Tentatively she reached out to him with her mind and his thoughts embraced her with warmth that only true love could describe.

"Are you feeling better?" he asked her, showing just a little bit of anxiety in his voice.

"Yes, I'm fine. Yesterday must have been too much for me. I passed out after pushing you away."

"I thought as much, I've never been pushed so hard before and I knew you had done it with everything you had. Where were you?"

She heard his question echoing in her head but was distracted by another noise outside her little flat. There was always some noise or other sounds either coming from the street outside or on the stairs, so ignoring it, Maria focused on Anthony and answered his question.

"I was at work and had to hide in a broom cupboard then I passed out. I was woken by one of the hospital cleaners.

Luckily enough I had told her I was reaching for a bucket and it had fallen on my head."

Anthony was laughing hard as he imagined the scene.

"Thank you for saving my life yesterday, I suppose that makes us even?"

"I suppose it does. Well, at least you are ok." she replied.

Just then, there was another scuffling noise outside and then again it stopped.

Anthony continued. "There was something strange about yesterday, everything got worse when I arrived back with my company. I know this sounds like I'm paranoid but it seemed like they were attacking to kill me."

Maria went silent for a second, and then asked Anthony something. "You don't really think that do you?" suddenly feeling scared for him.

"Not really, but since yesterday there have been some translations of papers found on dead soldiers that sounded like they were trying to capture me, as if I was the target of the attack."

Maria thought about this for another moment but couldn't understand why the Germans would want to capture Anthony.

"Please be careful Anthony I don't want anything bad to happen to you. I have to go, I'm working the night shift and I'm late already. I love you!"

"I love you too. Be careful yourself."

CHAPTER 9   MY SOUL IS CAPTURED

Maria left her flat, and locked the door behind her and walked downstairs. The building was quite old and had been recently fitted out as a residence for University students but when the Second World War had started it had been used for to house nurses. Maria normally shared her flat with another nurse but she had gone over to France so and she had the flat to herself.

Walking out onto the street Maria noticed that it was busier than usual, but paid no attention to anyone. Everyone during the war kept to themselves and didn't socialise as much as they used to. The faces Maria recognised near her home were the only ones she would say "Good evening" to and even then she wouldn't stop to chat. She didn't notice the woman in a grey dress watching as she left her flat and then start to follow as Maria moved off down the street on her way to the hospital.

It was at least a twenty minute walk from her flat to the hospital but the day had been nice although the evening had a slight chill, a definite sign that winter was on its way. Maria stopped briefly to look in a shop window that had brought in stockings, real stockings that she hadn't seen in such a long time, however, they were too expensive for her to buy so she moved on. If Maria had just looked to one side she might have seen the woman in grey talking to a man in a car. They finished and the car drove off. There was a place where Maria would cut through between two buildings, being able to cut short the trip to the hospital by five minutes. As per usual she took the short cut and the woman moved closer. The woman in grey reached into her purse and pulled out a handkerchief, holding it carefully cupped in one hand she moved closer still to Maria as she was about to reach the end of the alleyway. Maria didn't see it coming; the woman in grey grabbed her from behind and placed the chloroform doused handkerchief over her nose and mouth. Maria breathed in heavily to scream but nothing came out as she immediately fell under the effects of the drug. The car driven by the man stopped and Maria was bustled into the back seat. The screech of rubber echoed down the alley and then silence covered whatever traces had been left.

Maria woke up feeling groggy. She had no idea where she was but there was a definite salty smell in the atmosphere. In the dark she could just make out three other figures, they stirred and she called out to them.

"Who's there?"

"Hello," a weak voice came back. "My name's Maria, who are you?"

"That's funny," said another voice in the background. "I'm called Maria too. Isn't that a coincidence?"

Maria was shocked and without asking she knew that the other person who hadn't spoken yet would also have the same name. She tried to open a connection between herself and Anthony but she still felt groggy and couldn't concentrate enough, so she decided to wait a little longer for the effect to subside and learn a little more about where they were and who had done this. Either way she had been captured and was being taken somewhere near the sea. Maria tried to control her fear but was really afraid of what was going to happen next. She breathed deeply, hyperventilating to free her head of the cloud fogging her thoughts. The other nurse was stirring and Maria asked her if she was ok. The nurse replied that she was.

"Just out of curiosity your name isn't Maria is it?"

The woman took a second to answer. "No it isn't, it's Bonnie. Why are you asking if my name is Maria?"

"For no reason, it's just the others and I are all called Maria."

"Oh, where are we?" one of the other women asked.

"We don't know for sure but it seems we are on a boat." her voice was weak and she was obviously seasick.

"What happened to us?" she asked with a panic in her voice. "My mother is going to be worried, I left for the hospital this morning and I was attacked and then the next thing I know is that I'm here with you three."

Maria asked her a question, "Did you just say you work in a hospital?"

"Yes, I have worked in the hospital since I left school last year. I don't like it but I suppose we have to do our part for the war."

The other two women owned up to also being nurses. Now the situation was much direr than Maria had thought; three women, about the same age, same name and nurses. Who didn't fit into the equation was Bonnie.

Maria was feeling a little bit better and was just about to reach out to Anthony when a door opened and light flooded into the dark room. The four women reflexively covered their eyes against the bright light coming in. After their eyes adjusted they distinguished a silhouette standing there, it was the woman in grey. She came into the room and walked over to one of the others and grabbed her by the hair and pulled her head back, the nurse gritted her teeth but screamed out loud at the pain it caused. Seeing the nurse's face in the light coming from the doorway she lifted her up and dragged her to the exit. Maria loved what happened next; just as they got to the doorway the nurse jammed her hands on the door jamb stopping the pair of them suddenly. The woman in grey was caught off guard and the nurse elbowed her directly in the face, she fell to the floor and didn't move. Just like that, she had been given a thrashing. Maria moved to help but just as she moved a large man appeared in the doorway and hit the nurse hard, just one punch and the nurse dropped beside the woman in grey. Maria froze and didn't move a muscle; the man grabbed an arm of the unconscious nurse and dragged her limp body to where the rest were back into their prison. Maria sat back down on the wooden flooring and as she did so the man turned his eyes upon her.

"You stand up!" the order came in English but with a very heavy German accent. "Are you going to give me any trouble?"

Maria shook her head. She wasn't feeling any better and she was struggling to concentrate.

The German continued, " Come with me, I have some questions for you and you had better answer them with truth for your safety will depend on them."

Maria followed the German out of the room onto the deck of a ship moored in a port Somewhere in England because she could hear people ashore speaking in English. They walked the length of the ship and into a large cabin which was covered with instruments, map tables and charts. He signalled for Maria to sit on a stool next to the chart table and walked round to the other side as Maria sat on the stool. He picked up a pair of dividers and stuck the sharp points through the map on the table, Maria looked at them but the room was swimming and she found herself dizzy, she had no idea why she felt so strange. The man answered her unspoken question.

"The drugs we have given you will wear off eventually but for the meantime they will keep you from doing anything out of the ordinary."

"Pardon? I don't understand why I am here or who you are or even what you are talking about?"

"Don't play coy with me, Maria. We have followed you for several days and know that you have made an interesting connection with a major fighting on the front line, his name is Anthony."

Maria tried hard not to show any emotion, determined to safeguard herself, her fellow hostages and most importantly Anthony. However, never having been in such a frightening situation, her nerves showed and her body language expressed guilt. Her interrogator immediately spotted her fear.

"I see I am lucky picking the right Maria at the beginning. This way I don't have to interrogate the others."

Maria wasn't listening to him as he continued talking about how clever he was at capturing her. Her mind was somewhere else. She had imagined a connection with Anthony but whatever they had given her, was strong enough to keep them apart. She heard his voice in her head but it sounded distant and she cried out to him in her mind begging him to help her.

She tried harder to concentrate and visions began to form in her mind, white rooms and doors all around. It stretched away into the distance forming a corridor full of doors. She mentally opened the doors looking for Anthony but found only empty rooms. She found herself pushing harder and harder, the drugs weren't wearing off quick enough.

"Maria!"

Anthony's voice was getting stronger and she had started to feel his fear but more than that his anger. All of a sudden every single door exploded from their hinges and out of one of them Anthony burst through. He saw Maria, he saw her fear but when he ran towards her he hit an invisible wall.

The German spoke to Maria. She didn't pay any attention. He spoke to her again. Anthony was getting closer; he was nearly by her side. The German struck her across the face, the blow knocked her face sideways but when she turned to face him her look had changed.

"What do you want of me Nazi?" Anthony spoke through Maria.

"Just answer my question. How do you communicate with the Major?"

"Well that is quite easier than you'd imagine seeing as you are talking to me right now! And just so know I'm going to kill you for striking Maria. Maybe not now, but very soon I will kill you with my own hands."

The German was dumbstruck; he didn't quite grasp the idea of speaking with the Major through this nurse. It took him a while to put two and two together but eventually he caught on and he became intrigued.

"So Major, how did this come about? Why the two of you?"

"It is none of your business, kraut! What are you planning to do?

"Well, for the time being we will be shipping these women off to somewhere we can keep an eye on them and you my friend are going to be very important in the time we will be sharing through are beautiful Maria."

"Obviously, if I don't then something will happen to her?"

"Of course, but that won't happen, will it?"

Anthony pulled back and let Maria take control again, he spoke to her quietly.

"Maria, I'm sorry this has happened, we should have been more careful."

Maria was tired but she had enough energy left to tell Anthony one very important thing.

"I have had enough with the war, now it has come to us and is affecting us directly I want nothing more than to finish it. Listen to me carefully before we lose contact again. You will have to teach me as many things as you can and we have to take this gift we have more seriously. Projections, defence and helping each other are all very well but now we have to think offensively."

Anthony looked at her in amazement; he had never seen her like this before, so strong and ready. He could see why he loved her so much.

"Right, there are several things we know how to do already, so I think it's just a matter of tuning them and practising with them. For now just rest as much as you can and we can think of a way to get you out of there."

"I'm not alone Anthony, there are three others with me and we must try and get them to safety too."

Maria emphasised this and Anthony agreed to try and fit them into a plan. He told her finally to rest and he left her with the German.

"Major or Maria?" he asked without beating about the bush.

"The Major has gone. I'm back. We cannot maintain contact for very long we both get very tired afterwards. It takes up a lot of energy."

Maria lied without thinking and the German shrugged slightly and had her taken back to the forward cabin where they were being kept. Just as she was being taken through the door, the German spoke one last time.

"You'll be glad to know that we will be going to Germany and if you do as you are asked we won't place you in one of the concentration camps."

Maria turned to the German and simply nodded.

"I do know one thing sir; pretty soon you are going to die!"

CHAPTER 10

THE BEST LAID PLANS OF GERMANS AND HEROES

Totally indifferent to Maria's threat the German ordered the boat to cast off, at the same time telling crew members to keep all four women securely aboard. He walked over to a radio hidden in a back panel of a seating area. He turned knobs and pushed switches to activate the new scrambling machine to hide his conversation from the British.

"Red Cross to Bald Eagle, come in Bald Eagle?"

"Reading you loud and clear Red Cross, what is the news on the new messenger service? Over."

"The new messenger service is underway and soon a full connected service will be available. Over."

"Excellent news Red Cross, we will be expecting details about Last Hope very soon. Over."

"Very well Bald Eagle. Over and out."

The German found it ridiculous speaking in code and even more in English. He supposed that if by any chance the British deciphered the message they would think it either their own or an American code. They had left the small port and were well on the way to France. There would be no difficulty in getting the women through enemy lines as they had all the necessary documents. A piece of cake as the British would say.

It took five days to get into a German controlled area and they were escorted from then on all the way to god knew where. Maria and Anthony spent as many waking hours as they could to come up with a plan. This was easy because all four women were kept separate from each other it gave her a little more privacy. Some questions had arisen why the others had been brought along. Was it leverage or was it just keeping the whole thing a secret. She Maria didn't bother to think about it too much as both she and Anthony were learning how much love they had for each other. They were channelling their energy back and forth at first but then bigger challenges arose. On the second day and when Maria was fully rested she received Anthony's energy, she was over-brimming with it and she tried to move the extra part of it down her arm to her hand. She felt it pulsating and could barely stand the pain it caused her, she couldn't bring it back into her body, it felt like it was stuck there. Instead she pushed it out and her hand lit up with a bright light, she slammed it down on the floor of the crate she was sitting in and she felt it surge. When she removed her hand the wooden flooring of the crate was completely chipped and burnt.

They continued practising and they got stronger. Anthony had another idea to try to protect Maria and the other women but this time it was Maria who did it first. She had sent her energy to Anthony but she began to "paint" the image she had of him with adjectives. 'Strong' and 'hard' were the first ones she thought and Anthony did feel stronger and when came through he banged his hand against the wall and it didn't hurt in the least. Over the following days Maria and Anthony grew stronger. Before they were aware of each other and began to love each other. Now they both wished to be able to touch one another, feel their hands and hearts. Maria had Anthony reach out to her with all the energy he could before losing contact and tried new ideas. The first was what she called, "Do not move me!" they tried this on one of the guards and for a brief instant the guard couldn't even budge her. She let go so he wouldn't take any notice of it. They became stronger. The next was making her lighter, for some unknown reason this was easier and used a lot less energy. She could feel how light she was becoming and at one point fell through the bed she was sitting on at the time. This one she called "Do not touch me!" It was surprising how quickly they learned these few things, Maria supposed this was because they knew so much about each other already that it made it easier. They had perfected only a few things but they would be significant in their plans for escape.

Anthony on the other hand, while Maria was resting, made other plans. He had gone to see his commanding officers and had explained the whole situation to them. Although at first they were sceptical they had no other reason to disbelieve Anthony due to his exceptional record, and to be quite honest they had wondered how he had done certain things and the news explained many of them. They had promised to wait and see what the plans were going to be and sent Anthony back to the front line awaiting news and, knowing that he was being watched, he had to be sure he was seen. For some unknown reason all the attacks by Germany had stopped.

The German had taken the prisoners through enemy lines without any problem, showing papers from the red cross about delivery of medicines to the front line, and then at night they crossed over a hair raising stretch of open land and made it into a German controlled zone. Once on their own side they travelled faster and arrived in Ardennes, five whole days after they had left England. The German and his men had hardly slept and had barely eaten.

Keeping the women alive and well was important and even though they had not left the crates they had given them food, drink and potties through a hatch in the sides of the crates. When they arrived at Ardennes they were taken out of their crates and deposited in small rooms, one next to the other. The walls were made of brick and the doors of solid oak. There were the usual things you would find in a small prison. A toilet in the corner and a sink that had seen better days, but at least clean water came out of the tap then in the other corner was a spring bed with an extra thin mattress and typical military style blanket.

Maria sat down on the bed and breathed deeply, it was colder in the small room but she was more than glad to stretch her legs. The confinement of the crate was straining all her will power to the limit. The others hadn't faired so well. One of the other Maria's had to be hit unconscious the day before their arrival because she couldn't take the closed space anymore. After that she didn't make much more noise. Bonnie hadn't caused a scene but a brief glimpse of her when they were pulled out of the boxes was enough to see that her right leg was in a bad way. The last Maria she knew nothing about her, other than they dumped her in the room next to hers. She had thought that the first Maria would need help and had convinced the German to have a look at her. After a brief argument in German she eventually heard the doctor going in to see to the first Maria's wounds.

A meal was served later on that morning and it was better than what they had eaten until now. Maria ate it feverishly, not knowing if there was going to be another meal any time soon. Shortly after she was brought before another German, this man looked deadly serious.

"Come in Maria; let me introduce myself to you. My name is Klein, Hans Klein. I am what you would call a friend, yes, I see by the look on your face that you don't agree with me but it is true I'm your friend. If you would give me a chance I could make your life quite comfortable."

Maria found her voice, it was a lot weaker than she had expected. "You are not a friend; a friend wouldn't keep us locked up in crates or small rooms. Would he?"

"I fear that you are mistaken yet again. I am your friend and I'm sure that your special gift with the major will make you both my best friends."

"Friends do good things for each other." Maria was getting tired of this banter; the small talk was superfluous and totally unnecessary. So, she told Klein just that and his face changed becoming sterner and more serious.

"If you want to be treated like the others, then so be it."

Klein opened a folder in front of him and faced Maria. He took a deep breath and started.

"Germany is not going to lose this war and if we can't control things we will lose it. The Allied forces have taken back most of France and the other strongholds of the German army."

Klein picked up the folder and rose from his chair and wandering around the room he continued. The German resumed, "However, we have just one last chance. There is a huge force being assembled 200km to the west of Paris and they will make a final charge on Paris and take it back from the allied forces. Your job, Maria, which is quite simple really, is to get your major friend to tell the commanding officers that the attack will happen somewhere else." Maria didn't bother watching him; she just kept her eyes fixed on the table in front of her and the letter opener that lay there.

"Where?" Maria asked quite simply.

"For the time being I'll keep that information to myself. We don't want things to go too fast, do we?" Klein responded. He continued pouring information about plans and contingencies but Maria was lost. She had quietly opened a link with Anthony and he appeared standing next to her.

"Have a look at those plans there on his desk." she thought the words but they sounded strong in her mind and Anthony just nodded. They had done this before and had the task down almost perfectly.

Anthony moved swiftly around the desk and peered over the papers, they didn't appear to have much relevance and he shook his head. Maria saw this and slightly pushed the papers to one side when Klein wasn't looking. It was good enough for Anthony to see that this Military push was in fact nowhere near Paris but to the North of Ardennes. By the looks of the armament listings on other papers Maria moved for him, it would be the largest push Hitler has taken since they took over Poland.

Klein appeared to be coming to the end of his spiel; it was Anthony who noticed because Maria had been concentrating more on what he was doing. He disconnected blowing her a kiss and pointing at Klein. Maria turned and faced the German and smiled at him. He saw her smile and asked her bluntly.

"So what do you think of our plan? Are you willing to help the motherland to gain back what we have lost?"

"Never - but it seems that if I want to live, I will have to go along with you and hope that the allied forces win."

With this the German's anger increased tenfold and he grabbed Maria by her arm and threw her at the guard standing outside the office telling ordering him loudly to take her back to her cell.

CHAPTER 11   THE PLANNING!

They had been held prisoner in the house for almost a week and Maria had met with Klein twice after their initial meeting in the office. The German had continued to try and mislead Maria by telling her their plans and every detail always lead away from the real plans at Ardennes. Every time Maria was called to see the German Anthony was always present. Maria was clever enough to keep quiet yet she listened to Anthony telling her that everything was going to plan, and she should keep throwing red herrings at Klein.

Klein on the other hand was keeping a close eye on military activity to the west of Paris and was happy to hear that a very large force had separated from its main base near Paris and was making a slow arc towards the place where he had been planting information. The whole movement of troops gave the impression of routine manoeuvres. However, they had placed their camp directly in line between Paris and from where the German army was supposed to make its attack.

Anthony told Maria that there was a military unit descending on Ardennes and even though they were moving in by plane, they would all be ready to stop the push through to the Ardennes.

This final push had not been prompted with the intent to attack and take back Paris, but to rush the French/Belgium border and take back the northern French coast, the Belgium coastline and the port of Antwerp. Then, once a strong coastal foothold had been established, the German army could begin waging direct attacks on England. The Allied Forces would then have to pull back and leave France to the Germans again. If all went well by Christmas Germany would destroy the Allied strength in France and by summer England would be under Nazi rule. A dream come true.

Anthony's commanders had organised a small force to counter this final push by German forces and there were more soldiers on the way. The small attack force will have to hold them back for a couple of day before a full force could get there.

"The Battle of The Bulge" as it would come to be known, was about to happen and thanks to a couple with a special gift, the Nazi final push was to be quashed. One final battle and

World War II would be more than over. Germany would have to surrender; they would have to stop the genocide.

The plans were going well and Klein had no idea of their powers or at least the extent of them. This final Nazi push was to take place within the next few days and both Anthony and Maria redirected their planning towards getting out alive. First and most important was to find the other girls.

"Where do you think they are?" asked Anthony believing that they would have been separated far apart.

"The other two Maria's are right next door and Bonnie is in the room opposite."

Anthony stopped pacing the room, he would normally pace as he was thinking while Maria sat on her bed.

"Bonnie?"

Maria looked up at him and his worried face.

"Yes, Bonnie she's a nurse too but I don't know why she has been brought here."

Anthony disappeared through the wall, and crossed the corridor and went directly through the door on the other side. Bonnie was lying there on her bed asleep. Anthony couldn't believe it. He spun on his heels and returned to Maria.

"Things just got a whole lot worse."

"Why?" Maria asked him nervously; she had never seen Anthony like this before.

"Remember one time you asked me about my family and I told you I had a sister."

"Yes."

"Well, she's lying on the bed in the other room."

"Bonnie is your sister?   Now I understand why she's here! That bastard Klein has brought her here just in case we, or rather you, didn't want to cooperate."

"She doesn't know who you are, I haven't spoken to her in a long time, and we always seem to miss each other. We have to make sure we get everyone out."

Maria nodded and thought about the best way to get out. But they still didn't know where they were. Anthony couldn't figure it out and they were still ignorant as to how many men were stationed here.

"Get a good sleep because we'll be making a move tonight. We attack at dawn tomorrow so they will have no use for you after that, there will be no need to keep you alive." said Anthony.

"Then we will definitely need to be out of here by tonight!

CHAPTER 12   THE GETAWAY

Maria slept, it was easier to sleep after being with Anthony and several hours later she woke up, washed her face at the small sink in her room, and tied back her hair in a high ponytail with thread pulled from the blanket. She was just about to reach out to Anthony when the lock on her door clicked and it opened slowly and silently. Maria stood there anxiously and was more than relieved when Bonnie's face cautiously appeared.

"What are you doing here?" Maria asked incredulously.

"One of the guards has been, shall we say, friendly with me and I took advantage of his friendship. He told me yesterday that they were going to move us somewhere better. Which I understood as, they don't need us anymore."

"That's right. Listen Bonnie, there's something that I have to tell you. I'm in contact with...."

Just as Maria was about to tell Bonnie about her brother there was a terrible noise outside, sirens were sounding and people were shouting. Maria cut off what she was about to say and they both rushed to the door. Looking out they didn't see anyone, so they quickly moved to the other rooms unlocking the doors with the keys Bonnie had acquired from her German friend. The other nurses were already awake and were surprised to see the two women opening their doors, but quickly rallied when they found out they were about to escape the hellhole. It was then they heard more noises and running feet coming in their direction. Maria quickly reached out to Anthony and he appeared by her side ready to begin the escape but found that the girls were already half way there.

"Amazing Maria, how have you done this?" he asked her with a smile on his face.

"It wasn't me, it was Bonnie." she answered him. The others looked inquiringly at Maria and then at Bonnie. The blonde Maria looked at Maria and asked her.

"Who are you talking to?"

"Yes, you weren't talking to anyone here." said the black haired Maria.

"It's a long story, but I suppose I can give you all a short version. We don't know how, but I'm connected with a soldier, a major in the British Army. We hear and speak to each other amongst other things, and he is here to help us get out of here.

Time is limited and it takes a lot of energy to keep the connection, so the quicker we do this the better."

All three women stood there looking at Maria as if she was crazy, they were thinking that her captivity and interrogations had caused her to lose her mind.

"No really." she continued. "Bonnie knows him; it's your brother, Anthony. We met several months ago and we have fallen in love because of this gift we have."

Anthony broke in and told Maria to call Bonnie "Ugly Duckling!" that way she would know that it is true.

"Anthony has just called you his Ugly Duckling. Which I have no idea why because you are far from being ugly."

Maria's words seemed to have struck home because she walked over to Maria.

"Only my brother called me that. He was always against what my parents did or said that's why I'm his ugly duckling instead of Bonnie. She's right she must know him. Is he here?"

"Yes he's stood here with us, but we don't have time to explain anymore. We have to leave right now or we won't be leaving at all."

Anthony led the way and scouted the route, they got to the end of the corridor without any problem but then they had to quickly hide in a broom cupboard because a group of passing guards had almost stumbled upon the girls and if it hadn't been for Anthony they surely would have been all locked up again. As they made their way through the building hop scotching through corridors and doorways all the women started to believe what was happening, there was someone they couldn't see who was guiding their movements through the corridors and avoiding everything that would put them in danger. This way they made it up the stairs and finally came to a room that they had all been in before, Klein's office. Here Anthony stopped,

"Maria, we need to see if those plans are still in Klein's office, it would be a good idea to have proof. I mean, if we can capture Klein then it will be all over. If we don't, then we'll have the next best thing."

Maria nodded, he turned to the door and the others looked at her questioningly.

"Anthony needs to get the plans so we have proof of what they are trying to do. He thinks that if it doesn't get stopped here and now then the war may continue indefinitely, it may even be that Germany can get a solid foothold again in France. We can't let this happen. "

"That will never happen." one of the other Maria's said. "The allied forces are much stronger than the Nazis. They don't stand a chance!"

Maria looked at the young woman and smiled at her outburst, these girls weren't in any way meek and mild. They knew that given the chance England, with the help of the allied forces, would push through. However, Maria had seen the worried look on Anthony's face in their conversations and she wasn't going to let it happen either way. If they could stop everything from happening here and now then it was up to them to do it. She looked into Anthony's eyes one more time and pushed open the door to Klein's office.

It was empty, there were no papers on the desk and it looked like the office had been turned over, ransacked and rapidly abandoned. Papers were strewn all over the floor and Maria fruitlessly rifled through them, knowing that the papers she wanted were not there. Klein had taken them, but where?

"Maria, you had better try and get out now while the chaos lasts. Anthony whispered to her. "I won't be able to help you much longer, ten minutes more at the very most. Let's go, there's nothing left here so don't bother."

Maria nodded and roughly grabbed the girls, who had been standing in the doorway. Quickly explaining that they didn't have much time to get out, they all fell in line behind Maria and rushed through the door at the end of the corridor into total mayhem. They had got away.

CHAPTER 13   MAYHEM

Alarms had been sounding for the last ten minutes and it had nothing to do with the girls escaping. As the German tank division had been advancing towards Ardennes, getting ready to make its push towards the French coast news was coming in over the radio that an unknown amount of American forces had landed just forty kilometres from where they were right now, and with the tank division just on the other side of the town and making its way north-west at a snail's pace, there would be a possibility of them coming together and putting a spanner in the works.

That was the mayhem that was in full swing when Maria and the others raced out into the courtyard. Pulling the rest into a group against the wall they avoided several soldiers running past and after that they tried to stay out of sight of anyone that was running by. Anthony was still with them and he kept telling Maria to either duck behind places or hide behind vehicles. They made it to the fence on the west side of the all the buildings, but it seemed like their luck had finally run out.

A searchlight fell on them; all five women turned and shielded their eyes against the blinding light.

Screams over the already noisy background were drowned out and even though the searchlight stayed fixed on them there weren't many people looking in their direction, Anthony thought fast.

"Maria, if I push some more energy into you I won't be able to stay much longer, but it won't take him long to get a gun on us and if he does that will be the end of you, I need you to project the energy I give towards the searchlight, like you did in the crate on the way here."

Maria nodded and raised her hand towards the soldier on the tower and the searchlight he had trained on them, Anthony moved behind her and pushed a little harder and she felt the energy surge as it had inside her small wooden prison. The others just stood there looking at Marla raising her hand as if she were about to wave at the soldier when all of a sudden a bright light appeared from her hand pointing towards the tower. The effect was amazing, the searchlight exploded into a shower of sparks and the soldier took the brunt of it and had slumped down either unconscious or dead. The girls were back in darkness and luckily the alarm had not been enough to call much attention. Maria felt that Anthony was barely holding on and she fed what she thought would be half of what little energy she had herself back into him. He visibly grew stronger and smiled back at her. She turned to see the rest of the girls gazing at her, mouths open and surprise written all over their faces.

"What on earth was that?" one of the Maria's said incredulously. "I have never seen anything like that before, are you some freak or alien?"

The others nodded their agreement and seemed to be waiting for an answer, but Maria wasn't going to give it to them just yet. Not until they were relatively safe. She pushed them towards a hut close to the fencing, it seemed big enough for all of them to fit inside and plan what they were going to do next. The door was open and they quickly moved inside.

"Ok, spit it out! We know that this Anthony is somehow helping you and Bonnie is his sister, we are all called Maria, you seemed to know where you're going, what you're doing, none of us have ever been here before and then to top it off you go and blow up the searchlight with a simple wave of your hand as if you were some kind of god!"

"It's not that I can promise you, it's a long story and we really don't have time for explanations. It's very cold outside and we don't have any sort of clothing to keep us warm if we are going to make a run for it." Maria pleaded to them trying to change the subject away from Anthony, but it didn't seem to work as they all just stood there looking at her to continue with answers to their questions.

Maria looked at Anthony, who was still standing by her side, he nodded at her and she took a deep breath and told the girls briefly what had happened so far. With every detail the girls expressions seemed to grow from disbelief to total surprise and then softened as Maria explained that they were in love and this connection they had was the reason they loved each other so much. After ten minutes they all held hands, smiled at one another and made a wordless pact to help one another to get out of the hellhole they were all in. Maria looked at them all and felt that this situation was bringing them closer together and she in fact loved them all for being there with her.

As Maria thought this, something strange happened, their hands grew warmer and immediately both Maria and Anthony's strength surged and neither of them felt tired anymore. The girls also registered this change and their smiles grew larger and they started laughing in the darkness of the hut. They had connected above and beyond their friendship, they had connected in some other level of existence, and they had become one. Finally, they broke free of one another and still chuckling looked around the hut they were standing in. It was a tool shed and there weren't that many tools hanging from the walls, there were some old overalls stuffed into a box and even though they were huge and dusty, there were enough for all of them and quickly enough they put them on to at least feel a little warmer.

Anthony spoke, "Wait here a little while longer. I'm going to see what is happening with the troops that have landed nearby." With that he disappeared and Maria told the rest that they should get comfortable as they had to stay here.

CHAPTER 14   THE GERMAN MOVEMENT

Plans had been going very well for the final counter attack on the Allied forces. False propaganda had been handed out amongst the Germans that were left on the receding front lines and of course they had been dropped and left for the allied forces to pick up and spread the word. These leaflets had the information that Germany was to make a huge attack on Paris and take back what was rightly belonged to them. It carried on to say that new German forces were being trained to further the war and bring it to an end with the Nazi regime controlling all of Europe and that the Americans had better be careful if they knew what was good for them.

All of this was a simple farce. There was in no way going to be an attack on France's capital city because it was too well defended. The allied forces had simply turned the German defences into their own and had made them much stronger. However, the German officers in charge of this counter attack had rubbed their hands together when they saw that over twenty thousand soldiers had been pulled back into the city and seemed to be making the barricades even more impregnable.

They also saw that the French/Belgium border had become less populated due to the coldness of the winter and as Christmas neared they knew that both the British, American and the other allies were about to make a fatal mistake and relax thinking that the war was finally about to come to an end.

Military officers had brought together as many tank divisions that were available and under the long dark winter nights had moved them into a position two hundred kilometres from Bastogne. This was a relatively long distance away from anywhere but perfectly reachable and once past Bastogne it would be a direct route to the Belgium coastline and that would be it, Germany would take back regain the upper hand in the Second World War and would more than likely win it!! The Americans will return to their country with their tails between their legs and the British will fall under the command of the Nazi regime.

With the order given the immense rumble of diesel engines filled the night, the vibrations shook the snow out of the tree branches and forest animals ran away as if death itself had arisen. Commanders pushed tired soldiers on foot to follow the slow moving tanks, occasionally allowing them to ride on the back of them, at least to get warmer or have a cigarette while resting their legs against the freezing nights. On many occasions fuel trucks awaited under thick forest canopies for the tanks to arrive. There was no way to hide the sound of the mighty machines as they travelled towards Bastogne; however, they had kept to back roads, off any type of track and in many cases across fields and through hidden gorges. It wasn't a direct line but it was the safest route. Slowly but surely, the German offensive was making its way to win back the war.

Look out planes occasionally flew overhead scouting out better routes for the tanks or checking ahead for any defensive positions that could be made by the allied forces. They continually passed the encrypted information over the wireless to the leading tanks and then the information was delivered by notes within their ranks. Fairly simple planning, the Germans had learnt a long time ago that the British and allied forces tend to see simple codes as much more than they really were. So, many times what was really happening was in fact what was in the real message, just adorned a little bit more with over the top descriptions and set phrases.

The faces of the soldiers, as they followed in the tread marks left by the tanks, were weary and depressed. Not because of the long journey they were taking, because they were used to travelling long distances, but, the constant cold. The freezing temperatures would be enough to take the joviality even from Santa Clause himself, the bitterness of the wind when they were passing through open areas and the deep snow as they pushed through gorges was definitely enough to wipe the smile off any face. Cleverly enough the soldiers had packed drums of burning coals onto the backs of trucks within the huge convoy so when there was a moment to stop these were fanned into a blaze and, at least for a short while, kept the freezing winds at bay. For several days now the soldiers had fought their way to battle but with no signs of fighting. They were losing their faith in their commanders and rumours were spreading that this push was madness, as they had done when trying to take Russia. It hadn't just been the cold then that had been the Nazis downfall but the lack of leadership and motivation of the troops. It looked like these stories of them were taking its toll of the German soldiers of now, if the officers didn't push them and on occasions shoot the odd deserter as examples to the others, then the entire offensive would have disintegrated.

"The soldiers are getting restless, my general."

General Von Kraft didn't look at the young officer as he poured over maps of the area around Ardennes. He answered him with an off handed remark.

"That's why we have SS officers with us to quell any, as you say, restlessness, amongst the soldiers. Go, spread the word that SS are amongst us and we should be careful with whom we speak, or go against the defy orders from the Führer himself." As this last remark was spoken Von Kraft lifted his gaze and faced the young man. Enough was the stare that the young officer immediately dropped his own gaze and quickly backed out of the tent mumbling something about following the orders to the letter finishing with "Ja, Mein General!"

Von Kraft was pouring over the maps and marking his army's movement.

"Too slow, we are moving too slowly, if we are to make this push work we need to be at least twenty kilometres further towards the coast."

Talking to himself sometimes made things clearer, but not this time. He threw his pencil onto the map and watched it bounce off the table. He grimaced slightly and moved towards the opening of the tent. It opened itself before he reached out his hand, another officer, this time one of Von Kraft's handpicked officers.

"Mein General, we are passing by Ardennes, it is just 10 kilometres to the south, spotters have been observing fighting and gunfire during the early evening and after it finally went dark. Do you want me to send a unit down to the castle to see if help is needed? According to information General Klein has a command down there and if they are having any kind of trouble we might be able to help"

Von Kraft paused his step towards the exit and briefly thought about the consequences of sending a unit, General Klein is knowledgeable to our push, he was briefed by the Führer himself to help us if need be, he decided as quickly as he had started.

"No, if Klein cannot sort out his own problems then I am not the one to sort them out for him."

"As you wish Mein General." He clicked his heels and bowed his head quickly in accordance to the respect for his general. He turned and walked away as the General exited the tent and saw the soldiers walking by. Many of them didn't look in his direction, but those that did look didn't even register who he was, nor did they salute. Their grey faces and wet uniforms didn't keep the cold out but the attitude made it worse. He turned again facing south, looking to where his officer had signalled and his thoughts flashed again whether to help or not. It was just then that all hell broke loose ahead. Explosions and gun fire shot high overhead. The troops started fumbling and moving about wondering what to do. Von Kraft knew exactly what was happening, he rallied the soldiers and they responded to the orders and pushed towards the attack. This was to be the last and final push of the Nazi Regime and it had come to a grinding halt. There was no way they were going to make it unless they got past this, if he didn't the war would be over.

CHAPTER 15

STOPPING THE GERMANS IN THEIR TRACKS

Everything seemed to happen at once; it appeared that the Germans were aware of the attack by the allied forces on the tank division and were planning to help them out. Radio silence was in place so the only way to warn them was to send troops out directly and hope that they would get there in time. How they knew about the attack Anthony was not sure. Now everything seemed to be understandable. Why all hell had broken loose from the castle where the girls were and why Klein had gone missing.

Anthony had told Maria that he was going to check on the troops that were landing just outside Ardennes, but what he didn't tell her was that in fact he was with them. All the time they were running through the castle and in the courtyard then finally in the hut, Anthony had been sat on the plane surrounded by American paratroopers. As he came away from Maria, he became more aware of the situation at hand.

"Two minutes!" screamed one of the American soldiers and immediately everyone else on the plane started bustling around checking their chutes and equipment. Anthony just stared at them. He had never jumped out of a plane! Even though he was military and an officer, jumping out of a plane was not one of the things he had ever relished the prospect of. He concentrated on the fact that he was nearer to Maria. He turned his head slightly to look out of the plane window and saw three other planes skipping along over the clouds.

He was roughly pulled to his feet by a soldier called "Duke", checked over and his parachute clicked onto the line above their heads which would open their chutes as they left the plane.

"The troops have already landed sir and they are already in place. Seems like there have been spotter planes flying around and we got caught out in the open." Duke shouted over the engine noise.

"Yes I know the castle has been warned and they all seem to be making a move of some sort." Anthony replied "The girls are safe and the plans are not where they should be. Klein's position is unknown."

Duke's face took on a puzzled look for a second the shrugged. These Brits are strange ones he thought to himself.

There was a green light showing down the plane and all the soldiers started shuffling forward. Anthony closed his eyes and appeared at Maria's side.

"I love you so very much!" He disappeared. She smiled and looked at the girls. "He loves me." she said.

Just as Anthony opened his eyes again he was at the open door and without waiting for a second he was out and falling, then the jolt of his parachute opening slowed him down enough for him to look around at twenty other parachutes opening.

"Oh my god!" Anthony heard Maria's voice as she appeared at his side. She looked down, looked at him, went white in the face and disappeared. Anthony smiled to himself and then concentrated on how he was going to land. He hit hard. Brushing off a bit after the heavy landing Anthony thought himself lucky for not having landed in a tree or even worse a broken leg or arm. He heard a grunt coming from just over his shoulder and as he turned Duke was there ushering him over to a copse of trees. There were twenty marines there waiting and as soon as Duke and Anthony arrived they set off in the direction of the castle.

Their objectives were two totally different ones. A whole command of marines were already in place to stop the tank movement whilst this small squad was to infiltrate the Castle at Ardennes, capture if possible General Klein with his papers intact and make it out alive. Anthony on the other hand just wanted to get to Maria's side and help her and the other nurses to safety.

They had landed just a few kilometres to the north of the castle so it was a short journey to the outskirts. As they grew closer they heard the noise, but had no more information about what was going on. They stopped for a couple of reasons. The marines wanted to coordinate the attack on the tanks with that of their incursion into the castle. This gave Anthony some time to get back in touch with Maria.

Meanwhile, the marines attempting to stop the German push across to the coast had set up on a high ridge. They could feel the rumble of the tanks rather than hear them and even though there was no light yet, dark shadows could be seen snaking along the valley bottom. It was going to be close. They radioed Anthony's team that they were ready when they were.

Anthony had barely got back with Maria calming her down a little, she was still a little white, but at least she had got over the shock quite well. The other girls were looking after her. When he appeared, Maria asked him where he was, but

94

Anthony lied telling her that he was coordinating the attack on the advancing tanks.

"I don't want you to relax. As soon as possible there will be someone there to rescue you." Maria wasn't listening very carefully as she was looking at him, he had appeared this time fully dressed for action. He was wearing full paratrooper uniform of an American soldier. He noticed her look and replied to it.

"I am coordinating with the Americans that's why I'm wearing their fatigues."

"Oh, that's fine." She said. "You look different, but I prefer your English uniform. This one looks too big on you."

Anthony blushed slightly and knelt at her side, he brushed his hand down her cheek and Maria closed her eyes feeling his electric touch. "It won't be long now." He finished and disappeared.

Anthony stood up and looked at the soldiers around him and said with a quiet yet very firm voice. "Let's do this!"

The squad led by Anthony ran through the tree line surrounding the castle. Confusion and turmoil was going on inside and he was sure that the soldiers would either be on their guard or they would hesitate when it came to confrontation.

From what Anthony had seen they were organising themselves to back up the tank front marching towards the French coastline. They knew that they were about to be stopped in their tracks, so they were making movements to help out their comrades. It was going to be up to Anthony's squad to stop them marching off North and snag Klein's papers.

Sliding along the southern wall they shuffled to the large opening of the gate. Just as they arrived it was flung open and soldiers poured out followed by a German truck loaded with boxes. Anthony and the squad waited a few seconds more to be sure and then slipped inside, spreading out and making their way to the main castle building.

Duke stuck to Anthony's back and kept an eye open. They stopped at the corner of a building and peered around the corner, there were several German soldiers surrounding a car, it seemed as if they couldn't get it stated. Anthony was just about to move towards them when suddenly every soldier dropped to the ground, Duke pushed Anthony passed them, noticing a small round hole in their foreheads, and glancing upwards he saw shadows moving faster through the shadows. He actually had to look carefully to see them properly. Another two soldiers were exiting a cabin closer to the castle. Flashes were seen and they both crumpled to the ground. Anthony looked again to see them being dragged out of sight, yet he couldn't see who or what was doing the dragging. He started to realise that these soldiers were much more highly trained than he was. Anthony, Duke and two other marines got to the castle wall and moved in the direction of the tool shed where the girls were hiding.

Gunfire broke out behind them and Anthony turned at the noise. Duke's radio burst into life at almost the same time.

"We are blocked out from getting anywhere through the castle. We need a new route, please advise?"

"Damn!" Duke replied. "We have to turn back and go to the castle first, sir."

"No we have to get the girls out. If we don't they could be found and then we will have a bigger problem." Anthony pleaded to the Marine.

"Sorry sir, but the papers you mentioned are more important right now. We don't have any intel of the inside of the castle. You do, so, we go back."

Anthony stopped a moment thinking out what would be the best way to get Maria, his sister and the other girls to safety and quickly came to a decision.

97

"Duke, you go and take the girls to safety and I will guide the others through the castle. Klein's office is on one of the upper floors. We will get the papers. You get the girls out. Just tell Maria and Bonnie that I will be there as soon as possible."

Anthony waited for Duke to nod at his plan and move out towards the main gate.

Anthony shoved passed the rubbish piled up at the entrance and glanced at the marines standing calmly, waiting to make a move. As he moved forward the gunfire could be heard and turning a final corner he could see a couple of marines hunkering down behind a low wall. Anthony could see, at the end of the corridor, a couple of soldiers standing behind an old MG08. These two were laying waste to the wall separating them from the marines. The old WWI machine gun was working fine and they weren't going anywhere. Anthony looked back down the way he had just come; a small broom cupboard seemed out of place. Anthony had taken a lot of time looking over the blueprints of the castle and he knew there were some secret passages. He opened the door and threw out the overcoats and jackets, knocking on the walls he hit a hollow panel, click, the hidden door opened and a long passage stretched out into the distance. Three marines didn't waste time and pushed by Anthony, disappearing into the darkness. A few seconds later there was a burst of firearms and the MG08 lay silent, never to be ever used again.

The Marines moved faster now, there was almost no other strong enough defence as they made their way through the castle. Anthony just followed at a safe distance, just to make sure they were going in the right direction. His thoughts drifted to what Duke was doing, had he found the girls?

Duke and the other marine had finally made it all the way around to the other side of the castle where Anthony had told him the girls were waiting inside a tool shed. They had met with a little problem on the way but they had handled it efficiently. They finally had the tool shed in sight but there were about five German soldiers nearby obviously unaware that the girls were inside.

Maria had heard the German soldiers arrive and it seemed they were packing their bags with other things than rations and survival gear; they were stuffing golden candlesticks and other valuable items inside. Then, over their shoulders she saw a couple of soldiers making their way towards them, keeping in the shadows. At first she thought it was Anthony and was about to project herself to his side when she realised that it wasn't him, this soldier was much bigger than Anthony. Maria moved to the side of the tool shed and out of sight of the Germans opened a small window. Duke saw her immediately and signalled her to be quiet by putting his finger to his lips. Maria nodded. Duke then continued to give hand signals to Maria telling her what he wanted her to do.

Moving his hand as if he was opening the door, he was asking Maria to walk out of the tool shed. Then using his hand as if he was making noise and acting the clown he pointed towards the Germans and lifted his Thompson Machine gun and clipped in a huge one hundred round drum magazine and slid back the cock. He gave the thumbs up sign to Maria and moved closer to the shed.

Maria had understood very clearly what the soldier had wanted her to do. He wanted her to be a distraction. Easy enough, but also very scary, she told the other girls to stay out of sight. She moved towards to the door, opened it quickly and, putting her hands up in the air, walked outside shouting out loud that she couldn't wait any longer and that she needed to go to the bathroom. She got the desired effect almost immediately. Every one of the Germans turned and looked at the beautiful young nurse walking towards them. They didn't stand a chance as Duke let rip with his Thompson. When the sound died down and the smoke cleared the German soldiers were all lay dead on the ground.

Maria stood there with her hands over her mouth; the other girls came outside and looked upon the carnage with the same look of disgust. These Germans weren't men; they had slaughtered many others, men, women and children. They weren't Germans they were monsters. Maria had known German people, friends of her mother's after the First World War and they were kind, interesting and generous. No, Maria relaxed, these were not human, and they had deserved to die.

Duke signalled to all of them to come over to where he and the other soldier were standing. Bonnie got there first and Duke spoke to her.

"You must be the lieutenant's sister? You have his same eyes. Where is Maria?

Bonnie turned around and pointed at Maria just as she came closer. Maria spoke before Duke could say anything.

"Where is Anthony? she said, looking from one soldier to the other. "He said he was coming to get us."

Duke lowered his head and Maria feared the worst. She immediately stretched out her feelings to him and realised that he was ok. Refocusing back onto the Marine she spoke a matter of fact.

"He is fine, but seems preoccupied at the moment." The other girls looked at her with questioning faces. "He is in the castle, doing something else." Bonnie noticed Maria's tone and put her hand on Maria's arm.

Duke spoke before Bonnie could get a word in.

"He had to go Miss Maria; he is the only one here who has full intelligence on the inside of the castle. He has to lead the others through to the papers."

Maria looked towards the main castle and frowned slightly.

Anthony felt Maria connect with him but didn't appear. She was with Duke; he smiled and relaxed a little knowing that the marines would keep her safe. Still making their way through the castle they finally got to Klein's office and, as was to be expected, he was not there, nor were the papers. The Marines were also expecting this and as they now had a better idea of moving around the castle, they spread out into three different teams. They didn't even wait for Anthony to decide who to go with. One second he was looking into Klein's office and the next instant he was standing alone, watching the marines disappear off into the dark corridors.

Instead of following them Anthony decided to stay back and he entered the office. There was something about it that didn't seem right. Last time he had been here it had been through Maria and he had easily looked around at the office and more importantly at the papers on his desk. Now, everything had been overturned and the desk was a mess. Yet, something seemed out of place and Anthony couldn't quite put his finger on it. He moved to the other side of the desk and closed he eyes, trying to remember the scene that had unfolded in the office. The door had been locked, Maria had been sat in the chair opposite Klein, all the cupboards had been closed and the wardrobe in the corner... The wardrobe, it wasn't it the same place. Anthony moved towards it and noticed that it was out of place, as if someone in a hurry had pulled it back without any luck and had had to leave it. Anthony took hold of the side and pulled it back, it was heavy but it slid with effort to the left. Just behind the wardrobe was a dark space and it looked definitely like a staircase. Glancing over his shoulder to see if any other marine had by any chance stayed behind, Anthony realised that this was up to him.

Duke, the other marine, whose name was Spike, and the girls, were slowly making their way back to the front gate. They had tried to find an exit in the area they were in but without success. The Germans had totally blocked off the doorway with heavy boulders and other than blowing the whole thing to smithereens there was no getting out. Spike had searched through their kits for explosives but they didn't have enough and grenades weren't going to get through, so, the old fashioned way it had to be, back out the front gate. All of this had taken just a few moments and just as Anthony was starting his way down the passageway behind the wardrobe the others were starting to make their way out.

Judging by the rate the German soldiers were leaving they were either on their way to help the German advance through Ardennes or running away from the losing battle. For the meantime, Maria and the other girls were having a hard time making their way to the gate, avoiding moving soldiers, search lights and redeploying trucks.

"Halt!" screamed a voice directly behind them and reflexively all eight of them turned and looked at the four German soldiers who had come out of a side tunnel.

Duke raised his Thompson to drill them, but all four soldiers looked at the beefed up marine and immediately they all dropped to their knees, throwing their rifles to the floor and putting up their hands directly in front of their faces. Bonnie, who was standing next to Duke, put her hand on his arm.

"Let them go." she said, looking up into his eyes. Duke didn't even look at Bonnie.

"You heard the little lady. Get lost!"

Not needing to be told twice the German soldiers, understanding Duke's gesticulations, rapidly rose from the ground and ran off in the opposite direction. They weren't going to get very far; there was no way out that way. The group moved their attention back to the gate. It looked as though they were going to be there a short while; German soldiers had set up and had almost blocked the gate with an old World War I transport vehicle. Its front truck and flatbed were normal yet its tank

tracks at the back were purposefully for all types of terrain.

"I can't risk getting you girls out of here, ten thousand things could go wrong." Duke said turning to the tired looking girls leaning against the wall of the castle.

"Don't worry Duke." Said Bonnie, "I'm sure you'll figure something out. Why don't we go inside where it's warmer?"

Both Marines nodded and moved in through the door where the Germans had exited. Spike closed it behind them.

Anthony had left the Marines behind and was still on the trail of Klein. He was sure that the German general had come this way as he could smell his cowardly stench. It seemed like Klein's passageways took him down past every office and room on the top floor and at one point he was not sure he was going in the right direction. He came to a split in the tunnels, glancing at the right hand tunnel going up and then the left one going down, he had no idea which to take. Standing in the silence he heard noises coming from the left and without further hesitation Anthony moved down the tight tunnel bringing his pistol up front of him.

The tunnel ahead was dimly lit with lamps hanging from the wall and Anthony carefully looked around the corner at a flattened area. The floor was covered with boxes and wooden pallets laden with sacks and other supplies. A door at the far end looked extremely solid and was locked shut with a huge metal bar and padlock. It was the padlock that was receiving a beating. Klein was stood over it holding a crowbar in both hands and striking at the padlock with all his might. Sparks were flying with his frantic attempts. Klein was so angry that the padlock was resistant to all his efforts he turned and kicked at the wall, the thud of his heel moved the heavy block of stone, so much in fact that Klein didn't waste time using the crowbar in the gap and heaving the heavy stone onto the floor. Bending down Klein grunted as he picked up the stone. He did not notice when Anthony came out from the shadows and raised his pistol at him.

"That's enough Klein, drop the stone and give me the papers!"

Klein didn't even turn around but the sound of Anthony's voice did make him flinch. He dropped the stone but directly on top of the padlock and the whole thing shattered into pieces all over the floor. The door swung open and a bright spotlight shone through, blinding Anthony enough to give time for Klein to grab the bag from the floor and jump through the door just before Anthony got off two or three shots.

Maria heard the shots ringing out over the open space in front of the gate and then she saw Klein running towards the German soldiers. She called out to Duke and pointed at the General. The whole situation unfolded directly in front of them.

The German soldiers were by the front gate and Duke, Spike and the girls were off to the left, then far off to the right, on the other side of the castle, Klein had come running out. Duke immediately raised his Thompson and levelled it at Klein's chest. He was about to squeeze the trigger when he refocused on the castle just behind the General. He saw the English major exiting the door coming after Klein.

The German soldiers also saw the Englishman bearing down on their General, Anthony had his pistol raised and aiming at the General's back. They all fumbled for their machine guns that were slung around their necks, Klein saw them doing this and dropped to the floor. The moment he did this Anthony saw the Germans bringing their guns to bear, without even thinking Anthony shot and kept shooting until his clip was empty. It was then that he saw Duke behind them.

"Get down!" Maria's voice had never been so strong in his mind. The sheer strength of her voice threw him physically to the floor, and not a moment too soon, as Duke's Thompson ripped through the remaining soldiers. The gunfire ceased, Anthony raised his head at almost the same time as Klein. Their eyes met, Anthony rose to his feet, anger growing, dropping the clip from his pistol and immediately slipping a new one in its place. The General saw the look in Anthony's eyes and clumsily fell backwards into thick mud. Anthony levelled his pistol at the General's head.

As Klein saw the gun pointing at him he moved the leather briefcase in front of his face and started whimpering. Mumbling strange noises and begging Anthony not to kill him. It was then that Anthony felt a warm hand on his and then another touch his face. He knew it was Maria; electricity flowed between them, the connection was real, after so many months of being together and not being able to physically be together. Tears flowed down his cheeks and his breathing calmed. Klein saw the major breaking down and thought he would try something.

"You see major, everything is fine, and you have your lady and who will know if you just let me leave. No harm has come to you or her."

As Klein was talking he was edging backwards sliding through the mud. The other soldiers, the Americans, had moved behind the major and even the other girls had moved to one side. Klein glanced over his left shoulder; the gate was just a few feet away. All he needed was the major to look at Maria and he would make his move. There was still a chance these stupid girls would be of use to him.

"Fine!" Anthony shouted. "Fine! Do you have any idea how much pain and death you have caused and would have caused if we hadn't stopped you here and now? Look at me General! Do you really think I would let you go? How could you ever imagine I would let you get away with it? Hand over the case, now!

Klein dropped the case in the mud and Maria made a move to pick it up. As she did Klein's hand snatched out and grabbed her wrist and he pulled her in quickly. "You see yet again major I have the upper hand. I think I will leave now and take your little woman with me! Keep the papers I don't care. The war is lost anyway. Time for me to make my escape, they say Argentina is beautiful this time of year."

Anthony opened his mind and reached out to Maria.

"You will not move me!" he thought to her quite clearly.

Maria nodded and as she felt Anthony's energy coming she applied it into her body and felt herself sinking into the thick mud. The General tried to move towards the gate, but could not go any further. It was as if suddenly Maria weighed more than he could lift. He tried without any luck. It was then he made a big mistake. He tried to get a better hold of Maria, moving his arm around her neck. Anthony thought to Maria again as the General was doing this.

"Now listen carefully and trust me what I am about to say. When I push every bit of energy into you I want you to change to "You will not touch me", and I will stop this maniac once and for all."

"You are going to shoot through me?" Maria thought back her eyes flaring with fear and she looked into Anthony's firm gaze.

"Trust me!"

"Now!" Anthony threw all the energy he had left, every ounce of it into Maria and as he felt his own strength disappearing and his arm starting to drop Maria phased into nothingness. The General's arm slipped around Mari's neck and started to twist away from her. Anthony's gun barked just once and in true slow motion he saw the bullet fly slowly out of the muzzle and fly directly towards Maria's chest. Fear crossed Maria's face as she herself saw the shot coming and closed her eyes.

The bullet sped on directly towards them and as when Maria had passed through the bed, the bullet didn't hit her but

111

went straight through and ripped through the general's shoulder. Everything happened in a millisecond and to the others nothing seemed out of the ordinary until Anthony had shot Maria.

The major had fallen unconscious to the muddy floor and so had the General. Maria stood there holding her hands to her chest. The other girls had thought Anthony had shot her, made the ultimate sacrifice to stop the general. But no. as Maria moved her hands away there was no sign of any blood or of any wound at all. It was as if Anthony had totally missed. Maria quickly got over her shock and ran to Antony's side; he was lying in the mud barely breathing. He looked into her eyes and spoke to her for the first time in many months with his own voice.

"You did it! You really did it! Good! You know something?"

"No, what?" Maria Answered kneeling in the mud and holding his head in her hands.

"I love you so much!" he whispered. "I'm very tired you know."

"I know, rest, take it easy now. We have won!" Maria told him glancing over at Duke who had the General in hand.

"Maria, can I ask you a favour?" Anthony asked her quietly.

"Of course my love, what is it?"

"Can you lift your knee off my arm it's hurting a lot!"

Maria shocked again quickly raised her knee and freed Anthony's arm. Which very quickly he used to grab her around the waist and brought her closer to him, he looked into her beautiful moist eyes and said.

"We finally get to kiss, I never have thought it would be like this, here and now, but actually it's perfect!

"I love you so much Anthony!"

They kissed and something exploded around them, they felt their strength coming back and when they finally broke and came up for air, they realised that their connection was no longer there. They had lost their powers. They both smiled at each other. They were fine about it, they was no need for them to have them anymore. They were finally together and nothing was going to separate the Soulmates of War ever again.

EPILOGUE

Not everything ended so quickly. The Battle of the Bulge carried on for a few more months after the attack on the castle. The Marines eventually gained enough ground and the Germans surrendered to the marines during the beginning of January 1945.

General Klein, although severely injured was sentenced by the war courts to life imprisonment in a secret location. A few years after the end of the Second World War top military envoys received a small note stuck to a basic information folder that Klein had committed suicide. Not many people really paid attention to it.

Anthony was promoted to Colonel and because of his injury, was given the Empire Gallantry Medal for services rendered to the country and an honourable discharge He and Maria returned to Cambridge, England where they had a family and grew old together.

Nothing ever happened between them ever again.

The End

NOTES

Notes on the Battle of the Bulge after this story happened.

Battle of the Bulge.
In December 1944, a major German offensive was launched against the Allies in the Ardennes Mountains region on the Western Front
On December 16, 1944, Adolf Hitler launched an audacious counterattack against Allied forces in the freezing Ardennes Forest in southern Belgium and Luxembourg. In the subsequent Battle of the Bulge—so named for the 60-mile "bulge" the German blitzkrieg left in the Allied lines—the Ardennes' American defenders were caught off guard as more than 250,000 German troops and hundreds of tanks descended on their positions. A lack of resources and fierce American resistance eventually halted the German advance, but not before some 80,000 G.I.s were killed, captured or wounded— more than in any battle in U.S. history. Seventy years after the start of Nazi Germany's last gasp attack at the Battle of the Bulge
Here you can learn eight surprising facts about the fight Winston Churchill called "undoubtedly the greatest American battle" of World War II.

1. Hitler's generals advised against the attack.
Many historians have argued that the Nazi attack on the Ardennes was doomed before it started, and it appears that several of Adolf Hitler's most trusted lieutenants would have agreed. Hitler's proposed plan (dubbed "Operation Watch on the Rhine") hinged on an ambitious schedule that required his commanders to thrust through the Allies lines and cross the

Meuse River in the span of only a few days before seizing the vital deep water port at Antwerp. German Field Marshals Gerd von Rundstedt and Walther Model both cautioned against such an unreasonable timetable, and the pair later offered several written protests and alternative strategies, to no avail. Shortly before the attack began, Model confided to subordinates that Hitler's plan "hasn't got a damned leg to stand on" and "has no more than a ten percent chance of success."

2. The Allies missed several early warning signs of an offensive.

Early German gains in the Battle of the Bulge were largely due to the attack catching the Allies completely by surprise. Allied commanders often moved on intelligence gleaned by "Ultra," a British unit that decrypted Nazi radio transmissions, but the Germans operated under a veil of secrecy and typically communicated by phone when within their own borders. Some American commanders also dismissed reports of increased German activity near the Ardennes, while others brushed off enemy prisoners who claimed that a major attack was in the offing. Many have since claimed the Allies were blinded by their recent battlefield successes —they'd had the Germans on the defensive since D-Day   but the American high command also considered the inhospitable terrain of the Ardennes an unlikely site for a counterattack. As a result, when the German offensive finally began, the region was thinly defended by only a few exhausted and green U.S. divisions.

3. A bad phone connection helped lead to catastrophe for one U.S. division.

Few American units at the Battle of the Bulge felt the force of the German advance more severely than the 106th Golden Lions Division. The largely inexperienced outfit arrived in the Ardennes on December 11 and was ordered to cover a large section of the U.S. line in a rugged area known as Schnee Eifel. Shortly after the German attack began, the 106th's commander, Major General Alan W. Jones, grew worried that the flanks of his 422nd and 423rd regiments were too exposed. He phoned Lieutenant General Troy Middleton to request that they be withdrawn, but the line was bad and Jones came away from the call incorrectly believing that Middleton had ordered him to keep his troops in position. German attackers soon encircled the 422nd and 423rd and cut them off from any support. Low on ammunition and under heavy artillery fire, some 6,500 G.I.s were forced to capitulate in one of largest mass surrenders of U.S. troops during World War II. In the aftermath of the defeat, a distraught General Jones exclaimed, "I've lost a division faster than any other commander in the U.S. Army."

4. German troops used stolen U.S. Army uniforms to wreak havoc behind Allied lines.

During the early stages of the Battle of the Bulge, Hitler ordered Austrian SS commando Otto Skorzeny to assemble an army of impostors for a top-secret mission known as Operation Greif. In a now-famous ruse, Skorzeny outfitted English speaking German soldiers with captured American weapons, jeeps and uniforms and had the men slip behind the U.S. lines and pose as G.I.s. The German pretenders cut communication lines, switched road signs and committed other small acts of sabotage, but they were most successful at spreading confusion and terror. When word got out that German commandos were masquerading as Americans, G.I.s set up checkpoints and began grilling passersby on baseball and American pop culture to confirm their identities. While they succeeded in capturing a few of the Germans, the roadblocks often produced farcical results. Overzealous American soldiers shot out the tires on British Field Marshal Bernard Montgomery's jeep, and one G.I. even briefly detained General Omar Bradley after he answered that the capital of Illinois was Springfield (the soldier incorrectly believed it was Chicago).

5. U.S. troops mounted a famous defence of the town of Bastogne.

The German push toward the Meuse River partially hinged on the capture of Bastogne, a small Belgian town that served as a vital road junction. The area was the scene of frantic fighting during the first few days of the battle, and by December 21, German forces had encircled town and pinned the U.S. 101st Airborne Division and others inside. Despite being heavily outnumbered, the town's defenders responded to the siege with cheery defiance. "They've got us surrounded—the poor bastards!" became a refrain among the town's G.I.s, and when the Germans later demanded commanding General Anthony McAuliffe surrender, he offered a one-word response: "Nuts!" The 101st Airborne would continue to hold Bastogne through Christmas, suffering heavy losses. The siege finally ended on December 26, when General George S. Patton's 3rd Army punched through the German lines and relieved the city.

African-American troops at the Battle of the Bulge

6. It marked the first time the U.S. Army desegregated during WWII.

The U.S. military didn't officially desegregate its ranks until 1948, but the Allies' desperate situation during the Battle of the Bulge inspired them to turn to African American G.I.s on more than one occasion. Some 2,500 black troops participated in the engagement, with many fighting side by side with their white counterparts. The all black 333rd and 969th Field Artillery Battalions both sustained heavy casualties assisting the 101st Airborne in the defense of Bastogne, and the 969th was later awarded a Distinguished Unit Citation—the first ever presented to a black outfit. Elsewhere on the battlefield, troops from the segregated 578th Field Artillery picked up rifles to support the 106th Golden Lions Division, and an outfit called the 761st "Black Panthers" became the first black tank unit to roll into combat under the command of General George S. Patton. As the battle wore on, Generals Dwight D. Eisenhower and John C.H. Lee called on black troops to cover the Allied losses at the front. Several thousand had volunteered by the time the engagement ended.

7. Weather patterns played a major role in the battle's outcome. Along with facing down enemy gunfire and shelling, troops at the Battle of the Bulge also had to contend with the punishing climate of the Ardennes. The Nazis held off on their offensive until dense fog and snow arrived and grounded the Allies' superior air support, leaving both sides to grapple with near-Arctic conditions. "Weather was a weapon the German army used with success," Field Marshal Von Rundstedt later noted. As the battle raged, blizzards and freezing rain often reduced visibility to almost zero. Frost covered much of the soldiers' equipment, and tanks had to be chiseled out of ice after they froze to the ground overnight. Many wounded soldiers froze to death before they were rescued, and thousands of American

G.I.s were eventually treated for cases of frostbite and trench foot. The skies finally shifted in the Allies' favour on December 23, when clearing conditions allowed aircraft to take flight. The subsequent aerial barrage wreaked havoc on the German advance.

8. Fuel shortages helped doom the German offensive.

The Third Reich's much-feared Panzer and Tiger tanks drank gas, and by late-1944, the flagging German war machine was having difficulties scrounging enough fuel to keep them running. The Nazis set aside nearly 5 million gallons for the Battle of the Bulge, yet once combat operations began, poor road conditions and logistical missteps ensured that much of the fuel never reached those who needed it. German infantry divisions resorted to using some 50,000 horses for transport in the Ardennes, and the Nazi high command built their battle plans around capturing American fuel depots during their advance. Allied forces evacuated or burned millions of gallons of gas to prevent it falling into enemy hands, however, and by Christmas many German tank units were running on fumes. With no way to continue the advance across the Meuse River, the counterattack soon crumbled. By mid-January 1945, their Allies had successfully erased the "bulge" in their lines and pushed the Germans back to their original positions.

Printed in Great Britain
by Amazon

76873323R00073